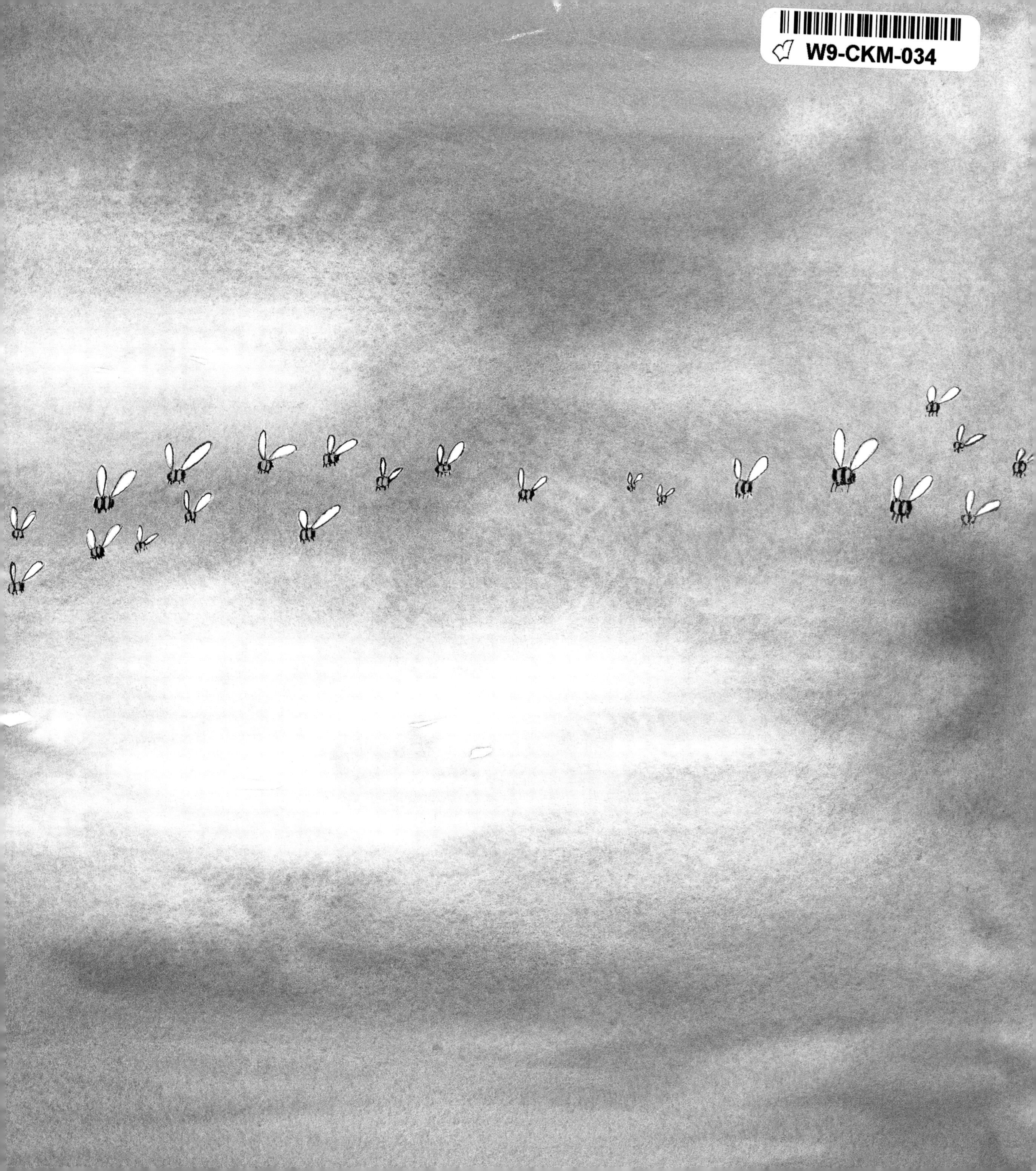

For Flinn – GA

For Cherry and Tony – VC

LITTLE TIGER PRESS
N16 W23390 Stonebridge Drive, Waukesha, WI 53188
First published in the United States 1999
Originally published in Great Britain 1999 by
Orchard Books, London
Text copyright © Purple Enterprises Ltd 1999
Illustrations copyright © Vanessa Cabban 1999
All rights reserved • CIP Data is available
First American edition • ISBN 1-888444-58-4
Printed in Hong Kong / China
1 3 5 7 9 10 8 6 4 2

Love is a Handful of Honey

written by
Giles Andreae

illustrated by
Vanessa Cabban

Little Tiger Press

Love is that highflying feeling
That makes you leap out of your bed.

Love is what makes you throw open the curtains
And somersault round on your head.

Love is that warm cozy feeling,
A cuddle that tells you you're sweet,

And love is that feeling of laughing out loud
When somebody tickles your feet.

Love's skipping out in the morning
And hoping the day never ends,

And love's what you feel when you all get together
And go on adventures with friends.

Love's when you hide in the forest
In places that nobody knows.

Love is that fluttery feeling you feel
When a butterfly taps on your toes.

Love is a handful of honey,
And love's making friends with the bees,

Even the flowers are bursting with love
When they're dancing about in the breeze.

And then when your stomachs are grumbly,
Love is unwrapping your treats,

And love's stuffing everything all in at once
Leaving masses of mess on your cheeks.

Love is splish-splashing through puddles,
And love's getting soaked in the rain.

Love is a rainbow that bursts through the sky
When the Sun begins shining again.

Love's when you can't stop describing
Just what you've been doing all day,

And love is when somebody quietly listens
To everything you've got to say.

Love is a great bedtime story
That takes you to faraway lands,

And love's when you want to show someone you care
So you snuggle up close and hold hands.

Love's looking out of the window
To wave at the Man in the Moon,

And love's when you whisper good night to the stars
Who'll be watching you dream very soon.

And then when you're tired and sleepy,
And you're cozily tucked up all tight,

Love is that last little cuddle and kiss
That helps you sleep safe through the night....

Good night